The Gypsies Spell

The azure blue Mercedes that pulled into the parking space in front of the old building belonged to Mark Stanley, who made his millions in real estate. The building he was entering was one that he wanted to purchase, a tiny shop called 'Witches Brew Potions'.

Mark had been buying up real estate lots on the street with the plan of clearing the land and building an office building. So far, the one holdout was the owner of this tiny shop, and after his lawyers had struck out attempting to buy out the lady, Mark decided that he would try to sweet talk her. After all, Mark was well aware that he had a way with the ladies, and few could say 'no' when he laid on the charm.

In fact, even though Mark was married, he still played the field whenever he felt he could get away with it, and he rarely had any problems picking up women. His wife Sophia however, was straight-laced when it came to sex, (where it had to be in bed in the dark) had her suspicions about her husband, but she still loved him and she figured that as long as he took care of her the way he always had, she would ignore his indiscretions.

Walking through the front door, an overhead bell jangling, Mark felt like he had walked into another world. It was dark in the store, the place seemed to be lit by candlelight. The walls were full of hundreds of bottles of different size and color. Down the center of the store there was one shelving unit with shelves on both sides. Everything looked either handmade or extremely old. At the far end of the store was a wooden counter and behind that was a curtain concealing an arched doorway.

There was so much to look at, but Mark just glanced around as he headed to the counter. The curtain was pushed aside as he reached the counter and a beautiful, brunette gypsy woman walked out, her large breasts were threatening to spill out of her low top. Mark was captivated by her stunning beauty and for a second, he forgot the reason he was there.

"How can I help you sir?" The exquisite woman asked.

"Uh, I uhmm' Mark's brain was completely flustered and he couldn't talk.

"It's okay sir," the gypsy woman said with a warm smile "you don't have to speak, I can read your eyes if you would like me to. Would you like that sir?"

Mark was thinking in his head what he needed to say, but for some reason his mouth didn't seem to want to work. Without even realizing what he was doing, he nodded his head.

"Okay sir, just look into my eyes."

That was a very easy thing to do. The woman's eyes were the deepest blue and when Mark looked into her eyes, he felt as if he was falling into them. He could have stared into her eyes all day long and when she turned away from him, he hadn't even realized that he had been staring into her eyes for ten minutes, to him it only seemed like a few seconds.

"I believe that I know what you desire sir. Your wife is reluctant to pleasure you orally, and you would like me to remedy that. Is that correct sir?"

It was the oddest thing for her to say and not at all why he had come into the shop in the first place, but he felt himself nodding again. It was true though. Mark had been married to Sophia for five years now and he often argued with her about oral sex. He wanted it and she refused to do it.

"Very well sir, you will need to come around the counter and into the back room with me so we can get the ingredients for your potion. Please follow me." She smiled sweetly and motioned for him to follow.

As if in a trance, Mark made his way around the counter and through the curtain that the sexy gypsy girl held open for him. The room he entered seemed totally out of place, not because of how it was decorated, but because of its size. The room was huge. Much larger than it could possibly be based on the tiny footprint of the store outside. From outside, the store looked like a small ranch style house and the front part of the store appeared to be the right size, but this room seemed at least three times larger than was possible.

"The potion that I am going to mix will make your wife crave your semen sir. She will find that she needs to have a taste of your semen every day or else she will have some unpleasant side effects. I will mix the ingredients first, then add them to your wife's favorite desert. What is her favorite desert sir?"

Walking two steps behind, Mark was transfixed with the sight of the young Gypsies ass. It seemed as if her entire body had him mesmerized. He heard her question and had to really concentrate to find an answer for her in his addled brain. "Uhmm, she uh...she likes apple pie. It's her favorite."

"Apple pie, how quaint. You are in luck sir, I just so happen to have an apple pie and all I need to do is add the special ingredient. Do you know what the special ingredient is sir? It is semen...your semen. You'll need to undress sir, so I can begin to extract the proper amount of semen."

"You ahh, you want me to...you want..." Mark was struggling because she had reached over and was stroking his penis through his pants, and he was uncomfortably hard.

"Take these off sir." The sexy woman whispered into Mark's ear while tugging at his belt. Her lips, hot, moist and soft brushed against his neck and he shivered, his desire at a fever pitch. His hands went to work, seemingly with a mind of their own, undoing his belt, unbuttoning and unzipping his pants until they slid down his legs and pooled around his knees. His underwear strained to hold in his swollen manhood.

The gypsy woman helped Mark step out of his pants and yanked his underwear down, letting his seven inch penis spring free. It stuck straight out at a higher than ninety degree angle. She grinned slyly and wrapped her slender fingers around it, feeling it surge in her grasp. Slowly, she slid down until she was kneeling in front of him and in one move she swallowed the entire length, planting her thick lips against his pelvis.

Mark sucked in a deep breath as he felt the most incredible sensation. It was the most intense deep throat blow job that he ever received and within seconds, he felt like he was going to cum. His mouth dropped open and he wailed "OHHHHHHHHGGGODDDDD I'M GONNA CUMMMMM!" He was certain that he was past the point of no return when he felt her hand grip the base of his shaft tightly and he couldn't cum. He was still on the verge, but she had effectively stopped his orgasm from coming.

The next thing Mark knew, she had pulled her mouth off his cock and stood up while still gripping his shaft tightly. His eyes bulged upon seeing her fully naked and he wondered how she had undressed so quickly. Her naked body was a vision of perfection and he allowed her to lead him over to an old cot up against the back wall. She had him lay down on his back before straddling him and guiding his ridged tool deep into her snug vagina.

Mark groaned when she released the base of his cock and sat down fully on him. His urge to cum had diminished. She sat still on him just staring down into his eyes and then began to use her inner muscles to squeeze and release over and over. To Mark, it felt as if she was sliding up and down on his manhood, but she wasn't moving her body. He felt the urge to cum again, but just when the feeling reached the critical point, her pussy clamped down super tight and held, once again keeping him from cumming.

"OHHHHHSHITTT Let me cum pleeeasee." He whined as the frustration built.

"Almost there sir, just need the right amount of semen." She said, her voice sounding heavenly.

When his need to cum had passed again, the brunette goddess began working her pussy muscles again, giving him the sensation that she was sliding up and down. This time though, she leaned forward and placed a plump, erect nipple into his mouth and said "Suck it sir, drink it all down."

Mark's mouth clamped down on her nipple and he sucked. A torrent of hot liquid sprayed into his mouth and his eyes popped open wide again. The liquid was sweet and when he swallowed it down, he felt a warmth flowing into his stomach. This was wrong somehow, but he was unable to stop himself from drinking in her essence and it was making him more lightheaded with each swallow.

This time, when Mark felt his orgasm fast approaching, he looked up into her eyes and she said to him "Go ahead, fill my pussy with your cum. You are ready now."

Mark was confused because she had told him that she needed his semen for an ingredient in the apple pie, but now she wanted him to cum inside her. It didn't make any sense to him but at this point he was too far gone to care and with a loud groan around a mouthful of milky tit, Mark exploded with the most intense, draining orgasm he ever felt. Every part of his body, from his nose to his toes, felt like it was cumming. He was screaming in agonizing pleasure while both brown nipples of the exquisite gypsy woman squirted a seeming unending spray of milky liquid.

The orgasm was so intense that when it was finally over, Mark was completely worn out. All of his energy had been spent and he was unable to even lift his head off the cot. He watched with heavy lidded eyes as the beauty climbed off him and walked over to a refrigerator that he hadn't even seen before. It was a tiny one, like college students typically use in a dorm, and from it she pulled out an apple pie.

He watched the sultry lady carry the pie to a footstool and set it down. From there she straddled the low footstool and lowered her bare pussy down until it was just above the pie. Mark was transfixed and disgusted by what she did next. He could see her bearing down, as if she was pregnant and pushing out a baby, and a big blob of cum, his cum, dripped out and landed in the center of the pie.

It was as if he was driving by a train crash with multiple casualties, it was disturbing and revolting but he couldn't look away. The first dollop of whitish cream was followed by several more, way more than Mark even expected, and at the end there was a funny farting noise as she pushed out the last vestiges of their mixed fluids. The last thing he saw before his eyes closed was her wiping her pussy with her fingers and putting those fingers into her mouth to lick the mess off.

When Mark opened his eyes again, he was standing out in the other room again at the counter and there was an open box in front of him with a perfect looking apple pie inside. Behind the counter was an old decrepit looking woman with wrinkles on her wrinkles. She looked to be not a day older than one hundred and twenty years old.

The old woman was talking, her voice sounding like the voice of a lifelong smoker, and indeed Mark noticed a long black and gold cigarette holder with a burning cigarette smoldering away in an ashtray on the counter. The ashtray was overflowing with burned out butts. Mark tried to listen to what she said as he looked down to see if he was dressed (he was), for the last thing he remembered was lying on the cot fully naked while the gorgeous gypsy emptied herself of all his juices.

"The pie will do the trick," she was saying "making anyone who eats it addicted to your sperm. One piece is enough to last a few days if that is all she eats. If you want it to last forever though, the whole pie must be eaten. When the whole pie has been consumed, the spell will be permanent."

Mark was looking around the shop, hoping to catch a glimpse of the stunningly sexy woman whom he had fucked, but he didn't see her anywhere. "Where is..." he began, before realizing that he didn't know her name "the young woman who was here earlier?" he finished.

The old woman who stood hunched over looked up into Mark's eyes and her face seemed to split in two as she smiled. It was the most horrendous looking smile that Mark had ever seen. Her teeth, what was left of them anyway, were as black as coal, and Mark could see the sunken depressions in her diseased gums from past teeth that were now just a memory. As bad as that looked, it couldn't compare with the serpent like tongue that curled around in her septic pit of a mouth.

"I'm the only one here sir." She replied and placed her bony hand over his hand on the counter, causing him to shudder. He wanted to turn and run from the store screaming in horror, but his legs wouldn't move for some reason. "The pie is fifty dollars sir, and I know that you will agree that it is worth every penny."

Pulling his hand away from her, Mark dug into his pocket for his wallet and, with shaking hands, delivered a fifty dollar bill onto the counter. He grabbed the box, mumbled a low 'Thank you' and hurried out of the shop, his legs suddenly in a hurry to get the rest of him as far away from the old hag as possible. As he rushed to the door, the old woman was laughing, or more like cackling, making the hairs on his arms stand up straight.

On the drive home Mark wondered if what had happened was a dream. It had definitely felt dream like, but it had also felt so real, that he wasn't sure. It seemed like such a preposterous thing though and the more his mind replayed the events of the day, the more he convinced himself that he must have hallucinated most of it. Of course he still had the apple pie beside him on the seat, but it looked too perfect to have been through what he thought he saw happen.

Pulling up to a red light, Mark picked up the box and opened it just a crack. He stuck his nose in and smelled it, thinking that if it really was full of his cum it would smell as strong as his cum, which had a very strong odour to it. The only thing he smelled at all was apple pie, and he was surprised when his stomach growled at the smell.

Setting the box back on the passenger's seat, Mark slid his hand down the front of his pants and grabbed his penis. It was wet and sticky and when he pulled his hand back out of his waistband, his nose was assaulted by the strong, unmistakable odour of sexual intercourse. It couldn't have been a dream, but it was too weird to have been real.

When he pulled into his driveway ten minutes later, Mark took a deep breath before grabbing the pie and heading into the house. He was still flip flopping back and forth on whether or not things had really happened like he remembered. He entertained the thought that maybe he had been drugged and led to believe that things went down like that, but that didn't explain why his cock smelled like sex.

When Mark walked into the house he called out to his wife Sophia "Honey...are you here?" He was peeking into the living room when she came around the corner from the kitchen.

"Hey babe' She smiled, looking down at the box he was carrying she said 'What's that?"

"I grabbed a surprise for you dear.' Mark answered and opened the box wide enough so she could see what was inside. 'I got you a pie. It's apple."

Sophia peered into the cardboard box and exclaimed "Mmmm that smells heavenly. What's the occasion?"

Mark shrugged his shoulders and said "There is none, I just thought you would enjoy it, but you have to promise to not share it with anyone. I bought it for you and you alone." He smiled lazily and winked before adding "Of course if you want to make it up to me, I'm sure we can figure something out." He leaned in and kissed her on the lips.

Sophia pulled back, rolled her eyes in an exaggerated sarcastic way and said "Ohhh...so that explains it. Your trying to bribe me so I'll want to fuck you. That's pretty low you know."

Mark tilted his head to the side like a puppy looking at its master and asked "Is it working at all?"

Sighing deeply and furrowing her brow, Sophia replied "Maybe...I guess it depends on how good this pie is." She took the box from Mark and said "I'm going to try it right now."

Sophia carried the box into the kitchen and asked "Do you want a piece dear?", as she opened the box and picked up a knife to cut it.

"No thanks dear, I told you that it is all for you."

As she slid the knife through the center cutting the pie in half before taking out one slice, she remarked "You're not trying to poison me or something are you?"

"Ha ha very funny." Mark answered. He was worried right now that she would bite into it and find it full of cum. He could picture her in his mind taking a big bite, chewing for a few seconds, then spitting it out and gagging on the foul mixture. But when she put a forkful in her mouth and started to chew, her eyes closed dreamily, she exhaled loudly and chewed very slowly as she 'Mmmmm'ed' until she swallowed.

""Where did you get this pie? It is fucking fantastic." Sophia said before taking an even larger second bite.

"I can't tell you all my secrets dear, or else I would have to kill you." Mark said while using a terrible Russian accent, which made his wife chuckle around a mouthful of pie.

Mark picked up the newspaper and pretended to read it as he watched his still sexy wife devour the slice of pie and quickly cut a second piece. She was a natural beauty who took care of her body and she had passed on her superior genes to her daughter Sarah.

When Sophia finished the second piece, Mark put the paper down and said "Well, I really should go take a shower." He stood up, walked over to her and kissed her on the forehead. "Glad you enjoyed the pie hon." He said before walking out and heading toward the bedroom to get some different clothes.

It was simply an apple pie, Mark thought as he walked into his bedroom chuckling. He had paid fifty dollars for that pie and he was well aware that he had been played, but his memories were worth ten times that amount, even if those memories were false memories. The gypsy must have run a scam on him and he fell for it, but there was no harm down. He would make another trip there, probably tomorrow, and this time he would be all business.

Mark collected his clothes, comfortable clothes to relax in for the remainder of the afternoon, and turned to enter the master bathroom. Sophia was standing at the door and startled him, he hadn't heard her enter the room.

"Oh shit hon, you jumped me." he said, then saw the look in her eyes, which was what could only be described as 'hungry'.

She closed the distance between them without a word and attached her mouth to his, driving her tongue between his lips and wrapping her arms tightly around his ass and grinding her body against his.

Even though Mark had just recently experienced the most mind blowing sex ever, his penis still expanded rapidly. He wasn't too surprised at his wife's actions because she occasionally became aggressive with him when she wanted sex, but still he wondered. His wondering was put to rest a little while later when she pulled back and breathlessly whispered "Oh God, I think I want to suck your cock."

At first Mark thought that he had misheard her, or maybe that she was just joking, she did occasionally have a cruel sense of humor, but when she backed up a step and began working on removing his pants, his breath caught in his throat.

The sudden realization came to him that his penis was still covered in sex slime, and he quickly pulled her hands away saying "Ah hon wait, you should let me shower first, I'm kind of sweaty you know. I'll be really quick."

But Sophia kept moving forward and said "No, I want you now. I want you...dirty." She had backed him up against the dresser and was back at his fly, her hands working feverishly.

"Uh wait hon I uh, I have to take a piss first." He was grasping now, looking for any reason to get away by himself so he could clean up, but it wasn't working.

"Oh please, you are so hard right now, you couldn't piss if you tried." She said as she finally got his pants open. In one fell swoop, she yanked both his pants and underwear to the floor, his cock flopped out fully erect and nearly bopped her on the head.

"Sophia wait!" Mark complained, but he watched helplessly as his lovely wife moved her face up close to his erection and smelled the thick heady scent of his cum dried penis. He was sure that she would pull away in disgust and start screaming any second now. His mind flashed through divorce proceedings and alimony, lots of alimony. He had been caught red handed after all.

Imagine Mark's surprise when his sexy young wife, who had up till now refused to put her face anywhere near his penis, was now sliding her nose up and down his length, smelling each and every inch, and moaning the whole time. He even heard her mumbling under her breath "Oh fuck it smells so fucking good."

He watched her in awe, amazed that she seemed so excited. How could she not smell the scent of pussy and cum, he wondered, when he could smell it from way up here. Then he saw her tongue come out and lick the underside from his nut sack to the head, before engulfing the head and the first two inches into her mouth.

It was happening. The pie worked, just like the gypsy had promised. So it had all been real after all. Mark was in heaven watching his wife suck him, and now he knew that when Sophia finished the pie, she would forever be addicted to sucking his cock and eating his cum. As much as she had enjoyed the pie, and she had seemed like she was nearly orgasmic while she ate it, he figured that it wouldn't take long for her to finish eating the rest of it.

Now, watching her suck him off for the very first time, Mark could tell that Sophia really was getting off while she sucked him. Her hips were gyrating and her skin was flushed. Her fingers clutched his ass cheeks and she was grunting and moaning and trembling. She was on the verge of cumming without even touching herself. If Mark hadn't just recently experienced the most draining orgasm of his life, he probably would have been ready to cum himself, but he knew it would take a while.

For the next fifteen minutes, Sophia worked tirelessly, trying everything she could think of to get her husband to cum in her mouth, but, although what she was doing felt wonderful, he was still far from cumming.

Finally, her jaw aching from so much sucking, Sophia pulled back and said "Does it feel okay honey?"

"Yeah of course. It feels wonderful babe." Mark answered.

"I think that I want you to cum in my mouth. I know it sound weird but, for some reason, I just want to try it. The only problem is that my jaw is killing me. How can I get you to cum quicker?"

There were two things that Sophia had never allowed Mark to do with her, one was oral sex, and the other was anal sex. Mark often thought that he never would have married her if he had known how much of a prude she was, but then the fact that she refused to have sex with him before they were married should have tipped him off. She might have been young, but her mind was old school.

Now that Mark was getting his puritan wife to suck his cock and swallow his cum, he thought that he could use that to his advantage to finally break her anal cherry. After careful consideration he said "I'm sorry honey, I know that you are trying your best, and I do appreciate it, but I've just got so much on my mind lately, I can't seem to relax and allow myself to cum. I think we are going to have to stop and try again later."

The look in Sophia's eyes was one of despair and she shook her head and said "But Mark, I really want this now. Maybe I just need to try harder."

"It feels really good but I just don't think that it is going to work right now...unless...no, forget it."

"Unless what? Please tell me. What can I do?"

"Well, I've got to admit that your first attempt at a blowjob is kind of...well, I know you are trying, but it needs work. I just don't think that you are good enough yet to get me to cum."

"So what if you just fuck me like regular, but pull out when you cum and put it in my mouth."

"Well, that might work, but I think I might even need more than that today."

"What do you need then?"

There was one thing about Sophia when it came to sex and that was that she was very naive. Mark had always looked at her naivety as a burden, and that was one reason why he went elsewhere for sex. But now there was a chance he could use her ignorance to his advantage and he was going to try.

"I might need to try something new and fresh, you know, to get the juices flowing. I was thinking maybe anal sex." He tried to look as sincere as possible while he said this.

"Oh! You want to put it in my butt?!? I can't do that Mark."

"Why not? You always told me that you couldn't suck me either, but now you are doing just that, and you want to swallow my sperm. You seem to like it a lot. So what if you try anal sex, just once, and realize you don't like it? Then you never do it again. No harm done. But if you do like it...think of how much fun we can have. And I promise to go slow and be extra careful. In fact, you can even be on top, that way you can control everything."

Sophia seemed to consider it for a few seconds before saying "But I want to drink your cum. How can I do that if...that's just gross."

Mark sighed loudly, then said "Yeah your right. Well look, I'm going to take a shower, and if you still want it in the morning we can try again." He stepped out of his pants and walked around her, heading to the bathroom.

After Mark's showered and dried himself with an oversized towel, he wrapped it around his waist and walked back into the bedroom, where he stopped in his tracks when he saw his wife. She was kneeling naked on the bed with her ass pointed directly at him. Her face was on the bed and her legs were spread wide. When she heard him walk into the room, she looked back and said "I found this." and held up a condom. Then she said "Please be gentle with me."

Dropping the towel to the floor, Mark moved to the bed and noticed the bottle of lube was between her legs. Like most guys, he hated condoms, but he could see how hard Sophia was trying, so he lubed his cock, tore open the condom and rolled it on while she watched. Then, he moved behind her where she couldn't see, and yanked it off. It slid off easily with the lube and he balled it up and tossed it behind him on the floor. His first anal sex with his wife was going to be bareback.

He put his hands on her ass cheeks and pulled them open, looking at her anus. "Honey, I want you to close your eyes, take a deep breath and slowly let it out. I'm going to help loosen you up, so it won't hurt when I put it in. Just relax and try to enjoy this babe."

Mark put a hand on her lower back and pushed down, causing her ass to tilt up, then he squirted a large dollop of lube between her cheeks. Using his free hand, he started rubbing up and down over her anus, not trying to push his finger inside yet, just rubbing all around. After a few minutes of rubbing, her sphincter was noticeably loosening and allowing the tip of his fingers to slide in.

As Mark continued to rub, Sophia began to moan. Her outer sphincter had loosened up enough to slide two or three fingers in easily, but her inner sphincter would need much more coaxing in order to relax it. He poured more lube down the crack of her ass and slid just the tip of his pointer finger into the tight ring of her inner sphincter. Feeling her flinch, he stopped pushing and just let his finger sit there while his other fingers rubbed gently on the outside, her opening tightening and releasing over and over.

About a minute later, Mark started wiggling the finger that was still in the tight vise like grip of her inner sphincter, and her felt that also begin to loosen. He could hear Sophia's uneven breathing and hear her occasional moans and he knew that this was getting to her.

Soon, Mark was able to slide two more fingers past her second sphincter and work them in and out. A loud moan from his wife alerted him to the fact that she was ready for the next step, and he used his free hand to pour more lube on his raging cock.

Stroking himself with his free hand, Mark pushed the three fingers of his other hand in as deep as they could possibly go and his wife made a 'UUUUUMMMMMMM' sound. He slid the fingers out and placed the head of his swollen prick up to her hole, which, for the moment was still wide open. His cock head was larger than the opening, but he didn't wait for it to close. With a slow but steady push forward, Mark slid his aching cock into his wife's furnace hot asshole.

"AAAAAHHHHHHHHHSSSHHHIIITTTTT!!" Sophia exclaimed as the thick rod slid into her most private opening. "OH HONEY IT'S TOO BIG!!!" She squealed, but Mark kept pushing slowly forward until his big hairy balls flattened up against her wet quim. "OOOOOHHHHHHSSTTOOOPP!!" She yelped, her hands balled up into fists clutching the blankets and her toes curled up tight, causing the undersides of her feet to wrinkle up.

Buried to the hilt in his wife's soft anal passage, Mark held himself perfectly still except for his hands which were rubbing her back. "Just relax honey, it's all the way in." He tensed himself, causing his cock to bounce inside her and she moaned again.

"Oh God, it's so big Mark, I don't know if I can do it! " Sophia wailed.

"You're doing fine babe, just breath. It feels so nice, it won't take me long to cum."

At that, Sophia groaned and said "Can you pull out and take off the condom before you cum. I want it in my mouth so bad, I need it." She was whimpering like a little girl getting a spanking, and her face was a mask of pleasure and pain.

"I know hon, get ready." With that, Mark slid himself all the way back until just the head of his penis was still in the tight ring of her ass, and after a second's hesitation, he slammed himself forward, slapping his balls against her soft pussy.

"HHHHNNNNGGGGG" Sophia grunted out loud from the first hard thrust, then she began a "Huh huh huh huh huh huh" as he commenced to pounding away into her ass. When he first entered her, she was sure that she wouldn't enjoy it. It felt like there was a bowling pin shoved in there and it was very uncomfortable. But something happened as he began to pump in and out, it started to feel good, real good. It was a shock to her but she went with it.

There was no question in Mark's mind of whether it felt good or not, this was the tightest fuck he ever had, and he was loving every thrust. He reached a hand under his nut sack and slipped two fingers into her slick slit. He was so thrilled with the fact that he was fucking his prudish wife in the ass and was about to shoot a load down her throat that he knew he wouldn't last long.

"Oh shhhhit hon, rub my clitty please. I want to cum so bad." Sophia moaned, and Mark didn't disappoint. Her clitoris was swollen and he found it easily, catching it between his first two fingers and squeezing it. They were both on the verge of cumming, and when he pinched her love button, she squealed in delight.

"OOOOHHHHHHHH I'M CUMMMMMMMINNNGGG!!!" Sophia wailed as her orgasm took over.

Mark felt her anus tighten up over and over again around the base of his cock. It was so tight that it felt like it was going to squeeze his cock off, but it was so good. He had to stop thrusting and hold on while Sophia bounced through her orgasm and he very nearly started shooting his seed deep into her bowels, but somehow managed to hold it back until she calmed down a bit.

When Sophia's orgasm was abating, her ass muscles clamped down one more time and Mark felt the unmistakable, uncontrollable feeling begin. "I'm cumming!" he announced, quickly pulling his cock from his wife's rectum. He didn't have time to wipe it clean, but he didn't see anything on it except clear lube, so he clamped his hand around it and his thumb over the hole, while his wife hurriedly spun herself around.

Having just experienced her very first anal orgasm, Sophia would have liked to bask in the endorphins and enjoy the moment for what it was, but when she heard Mark say that he was cumming, she became a woman possessed and in a flash had spun around. She knew time was of the essence so she pulled Mark's hand away and caught the head of his cock in her lips just as the first blast of hot semen spurted from the tip.

Mark looked down at his hot wife as she put the head of his cock in her mouth. The fact that it had just been deep in her anus seemingly not a problem for her. He felt the first shots of his cum squirt out and heard his wife moan. Her eyes opened and looked up into his eyes, then they rolled up into her head as she started to orgasm again. This wasn't any ordinary orgasm from her either, it was so strong that she began squirting a powerful blast of girl cum from her untouched pussy. Mark grabbed her head and shoved his cock to the back of her throat, holding himself there while he continued shooting sperm.

Sophia had no idea why she wanted (needed) to swallow her husband's sperm. She had ate the pie, it was so good, and when she finished it, she had a vision of her husband's penis in her mouth. Only it wasn't just a vision because her pussy had started to throb with the vision. She tried to put the thought out of her head, after all, she had never had the urge to do that, but her mind kept returning to the vision and her pussy wouldn't stop throbbing. Each time she pictured herself sucking him, she became more turned on until she had to see what it was like.

When she started to suck him, Sophia became even more turned on if that was possible, and her vision became him shooting his load down her throat. She had smelled his sperm before and had hated the smell. The thought of swallowing it would have turned her stomach before, but now it seemed like the right thing to do, and she was going to do it.

Then, Mark had surprised her by telling her he wanted to put it in her butt first. That should have been the end of the discussion because she had no desire to do anal sex, and she told him no. She even tried to put it out of her mind and go about her housework, but the visions kept returning. Then she remembered that there were some condoms in the drawer and decided that maybe she could handle anal if it meant she could get what she wanted (needed), so she agreed to try it.

The shocking thing was how good her husband's cock felt inside her asshole. So good that she had an orgasm that was unlike any orgasm she ever had before and for just for that short time she wasn't thinking about swallowing his sperm. But when her orgasm died down, and Mark said he was cumming, the craving was back worse than ever and she quickly spun around and sucked the head of his bulging cock into her mouth.

What she wasn't expecting was her bodies reaction to the first shot of his cum. Having just experienced a powerful orgasm, she never should have been able to cum again so soon, but the instant the sperm hit her tongue, her pussy exploded in a forceful orgasm. The pleasure was so intense that she lost control of her body and nothing mattered anymore. She was dimly aware of liquid spraying her calves and feet, and she never even realized that Mark had shoved his swollen cock deep into her mouth, blocking her airway as shot after shot of his sperm was blasted right down her throat.

Even though his orgasm was going on, Mark was still watching his wife. She was trembling like a leaf in a windstorm, and her pussy was gushing, something he had never seen her do before. He had seen woman squirt before in porn videos, but he often wondered if it was real, now he knew it was real.

When Mark's orgasm finished his cock became over sensitive and he pulled out of Sophia's mouth, but she continued to shake and her pussy sprayed three more times before she collapsed on the bed. It scared him at first because he thought that she had a seizure or something, and he got down to see if she was still breathing. She was of course, but she was unconscious, and her face was frozen in a mask of pure bliss.

Mark looked down at his shrinking cock and saw a drop of white cum on the head. He placed the tip of his penis in Sophia's open mouth and wiped the drop on her tongue. She moaned and he saw her thighs clench again as if she was having another mini cum. He moved around the bed and looked at her pussy. She was lying on her side with her legs pulled up and her knees folded so he could clearly see that her pussy lips were swollen, and the smell of sex was so powerful it was nearly overwhelming.

The bed was soaked from where she had sprayed so much fluid and he knew that the longer the blankets were on it, the more it would soak into the mattress. He pulled up the blankets on one side, then rolled his wife over until he could pull the blankets off. She was starting to wake up as he yanked the sheets out from under her, but she was unaware of what was going on still.

Mark checked the wet spot on the mattress and found that it wasn't that bad, he had stripped the bed quick enough after all, then he went back to Sophia's side. She was coming to finally and although her eyes were still having trouble focusing, she was trying to get up.

"Wh...what happened?" she asked. "W was I sleeping?"

"You passed out dear, when you came." Mark answered.

"Ohhhh yeah I came sooo so good...what happened to me Mark? I...I'm not like that. That's not me. Am I sick?"

"No honey, you're not sick. You just decided to try something new and you liked it."

"Oh my god, I was sooo slutty. I'm not a slut, I'm not like that. Why did I..." She was babbling and Mark leaned down close to her and whispered in her ear "Just take a nap hon. Just close your eyes and sleep." And she did just that.

Mark found a blanket in the closet and threw it over the bed and his sleeping wife, then went to the bathroom to piss and to wash his penis. Afterward, he walked back into the bedroom and decided that he too could use some sleep. He glanced at the clock and saw that it was only 5:30. He thought a couple hours of sleep wouldn't hurt, then he would get some dinner and relax for the evening. Laying down under the blanket, Mark drifted off to sleep and didn't wake back up until midnight.

Mark's stomach was growling when he woke up at 12:03 AM. He looked over to his wife and saw that she was still sound asleep. He watched her chest rising and falling in the moonlight through the open blinds. She seemed so peaceful so he carefully crawled out of bed and made his way downstairs to the kitchen where he nuked some leftovers in the microwave and sat down in front of the TV to eat.

The TV was on some action movie with guns and gangsters and damsels in distress, but Mark's mind was on what happened earlier. It all seemed like a dream now, a very vivid, intense, insane dream, but surely it was too outlandish to be real. But he knew that it was real, unless of course he was in a coma in a hospital somewhere and all of this was some hallucination. If it was a dream though, he didn't want it to end.

Before he knew it, it was 3:00 AM and Mark could feel himself drifting, so he got up, went to the kitchen to take care of his plate, and checked the fridge to make sure the pie was still there, it was. Then he made his way back upstairs and went to bed, falling asleep almost as soon as his head hit the pillow.

He didn't wake up again until 10:00AM and was surprised that Sophia hadn't woke him earlier considering that she wasn't in bed anymore. He got up and threw his robe on, and after a piss and splashing some water on his face, he headed downstairs.

He heard voices coming from the kitchen and recognized his daughters and Sophia's voices, and his heart skipped a beat when he heard a third female voice saying "Mrs. Stanley you were right, this is the best apple pie I've ever ate."

Mark hurried down the last three steps and around the corner to the kitchen where his wife, her bestie Sarah and her lesbian girlfriend were all seated around the island with empty plates in front of them. The color drained from his face when he saw the empty pie box crushed flat in the trash.

"Mark!!" Sarah yelled when she saw him standing in the doorway. She jumped off the high bar stool and rushed around the island to him where she threw her arms around him in a big bear hug. "I missed you so much." She said, kissing him on his unshaven cheek. Before she pulled away from him, he thought he felt her push her pelvis against his penis. It was almost imperceptible, and he wouldn't have thought twice about it normally.

Sarah pulled away from him and looked at him with a concerned look "Do you feel alright? You look awful pale. Are you feverish?" She put her hand up on his forehead, but Mark was still in shock. He wasn't feverish, he was freaking out.

It took Mark a few seconds to clear his brain enough to answer "Uh I'm fine honey, I'm just surprised to see you. You and

Marissa. I didn't know you were coming to visit." He felt a sickness in the pit of his stomach, but it wasn't caused by a virus.

"I thought it would be a nice surprise honey." Sophia said. "She called yesterday and asked if they could come for the long weekend. I said it would be a great surprise. Aren't you glad?"

"Uh yeah, yeah of course I happy to see you. Marissa, it's good to see you to. How is your family?"

"They are good Mr. S. thanks for asking."

"Call me Mark hon." Mark was making small talk but his mind was plotting his day. He needed to get back to the shop as soon as possible, before his wife's friend and her girlfriend started having visions like Sophia did last night. It might already be too late, after all, it worked pretty quickly on his wife last night. "Look, I do want to spend some time with you, both of you, but I need to take care of some business first. I should be back by early this afternoon and we can do something."

"Sure thing Mark, it will give us a chance to get settled in and showered. Oh, and if you can grab another one of those apple pies when you are out, you should. That one was so good that we polished it off for breakfast."

"I'll see what I can do hon. I'm going to go get dressed and head out." Mark headed back upstairs taking them two at a time and rushed around getting dressed. As he was buttoning up his shirt, he felt someone behind him and turned around to see that Marissa was standing in the doorway. She had a distraught look on her face.

"Marissa, are you alright?" Mark asked, afraid of what her answer would be.

"I...I'm looking for the bathroom." She answered.

"Down the hallway, first door on the left." Mark directed, turning back toward the mirror to finish buttoning. He could see from her reflection in the mirror that she was still standing in the doorway. "Is there anything else you need Marissa?" He asked, his voice cracking.

There was no answer, then after a painful pause she said "Ahh I...no that's all." and she quickly rushed down the hall to the bathroom.

Mark knew that he needed to leave quickly before things got out of hand, so he didn't bother with a tie, instead he just threw on his suit jacket and ran his hand through his hair. This wasn't going to be a normal business run anyway, so he wasn't worried about that.

As Mark hurried out into the hallway, he literally ran right into Sarah. "Oh I'm sorry honey, are you alright?" He asked, holding her arm. He noticed that she looked at him funny, just like Marissa had minutes ago.

Sarah looked down at his hand holding her arm, then her eyes went to the front of his pants, and she squeezed her legs together as a spasm shot through her pussy. It wasn't quite the same spasm as an orgasm, but it was hard to ignore. Her mouth was suddenly watering and her knees felt weak. Her mind was picturing her on her knees with his cock in her mouth and she didn't know why.

Just then, the bathroom door opened and Marissa stepped out into the hallway. Sarah pulled her attention away from her father's pants and moved around him without saying a word. She grabbed Marissa's arm and led her into the spare bedroom, closing the door behind her.

Mark exhaled loudly and rushed down the stairs. He didn't stop at the kitchen to tell his wife he was leaving, he just headed for the front door.

Fifteen minutes later, he parked in the same parking spot as he did the day before, although this time his car was crooked in the space, and hurried inside. This time he didn't take time to check out the store upon entering, he headed directly to the counter and rang the bell six times. He waited about three seconds then rang the bell several more times, until the curtain was pushed aside and the beautiful gypsy woman stepped up behind the counter.

"Hello again sir. How can I help you today?" She asked.

"I've got big problems lady. I need the antidote for that pie you gave me, and I need it right now."

"Antidote. I'm afraid that I don't understand sir."

Mark could feel his blood pressure spiking as his anger rose. "Look, I need something, a spell or a friggin' potion or whatever the hell you call it, to reverse the effects of the apple pie that you gave me yesterday."

"Has your wife eaten all the pie already sir?"

"Yes no no she ate some yes, but then her friend and her girlfriend came home and ate some and..."

"Oh my, did they eat the entire pie sir?"

"Yes yes it's all gone. What does it matter? Just make me something to fix this mess. Please"

"I'm sorry sir. It is impossible."

"What do mean it is impossible? I told you that my fucking friend ate the pie, and her girlfriend. You have to help me." Mark felt like he was going to pass out.

"Sir, look into my eyes sir." She put her hand on his cheek and his eyes met hers, her beautiful eyes, her deep, sensuous, sexy eyes, and he was lost in those eyes. His heart slowed down and his stress seeped away. The tenseness in his muscles vanished and he suddenly felt relaxed and at ease again.

When they finally broke eye contact, the sexy gypsy said "I can see that this is very stressful for you sir, but you must realize that what is done is done. Your friend, her friend, and your wife have all eaten the pie, therefore, they all will need to drink your seed once a day from now on or..."

"Or what? What will happen if they don't?" Mark said. He had calmed down a lot, but was still upset.

"They will suffer greatly sir. You cannot allow them to suffer."

"Alright, so what if I masturbate into a glass and mix it with their food, like you did with the pie?"

"I'm afraid that won't work sir, they all need your semen directly from you, and they all need the full amount, or they will not be satisfied."

Mark leaned in close and grabbed her hand. Speaking in a hushed tone he said "I cannot allow my friends to...to suck my...Jesus I can't even say it. She's my wife's bestie for Christ sakes."

"Your wifes best friend is how old sir?"

"Nineteen"

"Then she is not underage sir, and she needs you now more than ever."

"But it's all fucking wrong. Look, there must be something, some way you can help. I can't go home and" lowered his voice to a whisper again as if someone else was in the place "I can't go home and have sex with my wife's bestie for Christ sakes"

"Do you love your wife sir?"

"What kind of question is that? Of course I love my wife, but I don't want to have sex with her friend. My God what will my wife think? She'll leave me for sure and keep the house."

"Your wife ate the pie also sir, she will only care about getting her daily fix. In fact all three women who ate the pie will only be sexually satisfied by your semen. Only by swallowing your semen."

Mark thought about how intense his wife came when he shot into her mouth and a vision of her young friend doing the same crossed his mind causing him to shudder. "The friend is a...a lesbian, and her friend is her lover."

The gypsy woman brushed her long hair away from her face and said "I suppose that I can give you something that will allow them to still pleasure each other and you will need a boost most likely. Having one woman addicted to your sperm is okay, having three will drain you much too quickly. You should come out back with me to get a potion to help you stay strong."

This was all way too much for Mark to take in. He could see his whole life falling apart, his wife, her friend, both hating him but needing him and there was nothing he could do about it. He felt like he was going to be sick. He backed up a couple steps and bumped into the shelves behind him, then, as the gypsy began to speak again, he turned and ran out into the sunshine, bending at the waist and sucking in great breaths of fresh air, his stomach threatening to regurgitate all the leftovers he ate at midnight.

He contemplated not even going home, just getting in his car and driving away, never to return, but the words of the gypsy kept rattling around in his head. They would all suffer if he didn't give them what they needed, and he couldn't live with himself knowing that his little love of his life was suffering and he had the cure within him. In the end he drove back home to face the music.

Walking into his house, Mark didn't know what to expect, but what he found was way more than he bargained for. There was nobody in the kitchen or living room. Mark's office was empty too, but he could hear noises upstairs so he took a deep breath and headed up.

He stopped at his room first and found his wife masturbating on their bed. Her eyes were closed and her hand was busily rubbing away at her cunt. She was moaning and crying. He stepped back out into the hallway and made his way to the spare room that Sarah and her girlfriend were using.

The door was closed, but not tight and as he peered through the crack, he saw what he now expected, the two girls were naked on the bed locked in a heated sixty nine. Seeing Sarah naked, for the first time, he realized how beautiful her body was. He always knew that she was a gorgeous woman, tall, dark hair, flawless skin, athletic body with small b cup breasts. Sarah's mother was a tall beautiful Asian woman and Sarah took after her.

Mark also was well aware of how pretty Marissa was. Her body type was completely different from Sarah's body. Marissa was short, at just under five feet tall, and her body was more filled out. She was all curves, with large DD breasts and wide hips, she was the classic hourglass shape. The first time he saw her, Mark thought she resembled Anna Nichole Smith all voluptuous with a pretty face.

Seeing the two of them like they were caused Mark's penis to swell up in his pants and he backed away feeling guilty that he would get turned on by this. He made his way back to the master bedroom where his wife was still trying to get herself off. This time he shut the door behind him and made his way to the bed.

Sophia looked up as he neared the bed and she mewed, or at least that was what it sounded like to Mark. She leaped up and started to undo his fly saying "Oh I missed this so much."

Mark took her hands in his and pulled her away, seeing a look of despair in her face when he did. "Honey, we need to talk." He said, meaning to tell her the whole story.

"Talk later, I need this now." She whined twisting her wrists in an attempt to pull her arms free.

"Sophia, I did a bad thing and I need to talk with you now. This isn't you, it's the pie."

She stopped suddenly and looked at him, her face confused, but also knowing. "What do you mean, it's the pie?" She asked. It was obvious that she must have suspected something since she ate the pie last night and this morning and was acting like a nymphomaniac in heat all of a sudden.

"I went into that shop on Newburg Street yesterday, the only one in the way of the new development. I meant to talk to the owner about relocating her business since the lawyers had no luck. There was a woman there, a gypsy woman"

"Did you fuck her?" Sophia interrupted. Her tone wasn't accusatory, in fact the look in her eyes hadn't changed from when he came in the room. He remembered what the gypsy woman had said about her only caring about her daily fix and he decided to tell her the whole truth.

"I think she drugged me, or maybe she hypnotised me or something, but all I know is that I forget all about what I was there for." He was still holding his wife's wrists and she was still twisting and trying to reach his fly. "She told me that she was going to give me a potion, and that the potion would be for you, to help you get over your issue with oral sex. Honey, she put the potion in the pie that I brought home, the pie that you ate last night and Sarah and Marissa ate this morning."

Sophia's hands stopped twisting and she looked up at Mark again. "Are you going to let me suck your cock or what?"

It wasn't the response that Mark expected. "Honey, did you hear what I said to you? This...this is not you, this is the pie, or whatever potion or spell she put on the pie. You are addicted to my sperm, and now Sarah and Marissa are addicted too. They are going to need to swallow my, my sperm or else they will suffer...I don't know...withdrawals I guess."

This is where Sophia should explode in anger, shouting and yelling and throwing things around the room, but instead she said "I want it first. Do you want to fuck my ass again first. You can if you want."

Mark was so shocked at her reaction, or lack of reaction, that he dropped her wrists, and she immediately began to unbutton and unzip his fly, yanking his cock out through the opening and sucking him into her mouth. Frustrated, Mark used the last piece of information that he had that should get through to her "I fucked her. The gypsy woman, she sucked my cock, then she fucked me and when I came inside her cunt, she straddled the apple pie and squeezed all of the cum out of her pussy and onto the pie. The pie you ate was full of my cum from her pussy."

"MMmmmmmmph mmhh mmhh mmmmm" Mark could see her thighs clenching as she sucked and slobbered all over his cock. She had gotten better at it overnight somehow and she was devouring it with gusto now. He was rock hard now, and he was noticing that his cock felt worn. It wasn't painful exactly, but it was obvious that it had been used hard yesterday, and it felt a bit tender. It didn't matter though, because the blowjob was terrific, and even though he was upset by all the recent events, he closed his eyes and let himself go.

It took him 7 minutes before he opened his eyes and said "OH Shit, I'm cumming!!!" and felt the hot blast of semen shooting through his cock.

Sophia squealed in delight around her husband's throbbing cock. Her thighs clamped together and a shock wave of spasms coursed through her body. Mark heard the sound of water splashing and saw a gush of spray from between her legs. She was cumming again.

Sophia collapsed after her orgasm, huffing and sucking air on the bed, her skin flushed and covered in a sheen of sweat, her toes and fingers still clenched. The smell of sex hung heavy in the air as Mark stepped back from the bed and tucked his moist cock back in his pants. His mind still in a quandary, he turned toward the door and saw it open just a crack and Marissa staring at him. He heard a gasp from her and she pulled away from the door.

He quickly walked to the door and into the hallway to confront her. Closing the door behind him, he said "How long have you been watching us?"

"Just a few minutes. I'm so sorry, but…"

"But what? What do you want Marissa?" He had a feeling that he already knew the answer to that one.

"I… I don't know" He saw her eyes drop to the front of his pants and the look of hunger came over her. It reminded him of a movie vampire who sees a drop of blood.

"Where's Sarah?"

"In there" She motioned to the spare bedroom. "Please don't tell her I was watching you. She'll think I'm a freak."

"Why was you watching us Marissa?" Another question that he already knew the answer to.

"I'm sorry Mr. Stanley, I don't know what's come over me. I…" She glanced back at the guest room door, behind which was her lover Sarah, then back to Mark "Can we go talk downstairs please." She whispered.

Mark knew where this was leading, but he could see the desperation in her eyes. "Okay, let's go." He said, thinking about how Sophia had acted when he told her the whole truth.

He followed her downstairs into the living room, noticing how much she looked like a junkie in need of a fix. He wondered if Sarah looked the same right now, and figured that she probably did, but being his wife's best friend, she was probably denying her need.

The big picture window in the living room looked out to the street where few cars rolled past, but the neighbors were out mowing lawns and taking walks and Marissa saw all this immediately. "Mr. Stanley, can we-"

"Marissa, call me Mark please" Mark interrupted "We are practically family now."

"Sorry. Mark, can we go to a room that has a little more privacy please?" She asked, a pained expression plastered on her face.

Mark could tell that she was struggling mightily with all this and realized that she wasn't as far gone as his wife was. Perhaps it was because Sophia had eaten the pie on two separate occasions, where Marissa had only just eaten it a few hours ago. He thought about asking her why she wanted to be more private, but decided that it was difficult enough for her already.

"Uh yeah sure, we can go to the basement, I guess." He replied and led the way.

The basement was what Mark considered his man cave, a project that he had been working on for the last few years. He had put up Sheetrock to cover the cement walls, a drop ceiling with can lights, wall to wall carpet, and furniture. Being that it was a work in progress, he had yet to purchase a large screen TV. He was debating whether or not he wanted to buy a 65 inch LCD, or just go with the projector that hung from the ceiling and projected the image onto a screen.

Mark turned on the lights at the bottom of the stairs and said "Okay Marissa, what do you want to talk about?" He sat down on the leather sofa, a second hand piece that he had picked up from a neighbor who was moving out of the country.

Marissa sat down on the sofa next to him and placed her hands in her lap. He noticed that they were trembling. "Um, I, I don't really know how to say this Mr. uh Mark." She shook her head and turned away mumbling "Oh this is so embarrassing."

"Marissa, I think I know what you want." Mark said, wanting to help her.

She took a deep breath and turning back to him, she placed her left hand on his upper thigh. Shaking worse than ever, she looked up at him, her hand squeezing his thigh, and whispered "I don't know what's wrong with me Mark. I love women. I love Sarah. I don't like penis, I never have. I was with a guy once, in tenth grade in high school, and I hated it, it felt so wrong, so awkward, and I pushed him away and ran. I'm attracted to women, not men, but…" She slid her hand just a bit toward his crotch, it almost seemed like an accident, but Mark knew better.

"Marissa, it's okay, I know what you want." He decided that she had suffered enough and he took her hand in his hand and placed it on the lump that was his cock. "It's okay to touch it."

For a long while, her hand was still and stiff, just resting on the lump where he had placed it. Then, ever so slowly, she conformed her fingers around the lump until she was cradling him through his pants. She let out a long whistling breath, as if she had been holding it in for a while, and squeezed his penis through his pants.

"That's what you want isn't it Marissa? You want to put it in your mouth, and you want to suck it until it cums in your mouth."

She swallowed noisily and said "What is wrong with me? This is so wrong."

Mark reached down and unbuttoned his pants, eliciting a gasp from Marissa. She pulled her hand away when he began to lower the zipper, her eyes following his every move. With his fly open, he took her hand again, looked into her eyes, and helped her slide her hand into his underwear. Her breath caught in her throat and she shuddered.

"Take it out Marissa, you know you want to see it." Mark said.

She wrapped her fingers around his shaft and gently pulled it through the opening of his underwear.

Having just shot a load mere minutes ago, Mark was still soft and his penis had leaked a tiny amount of clear fluid, making the head sticky and wet.

Marissa was making strangled crying sounds from her throat as she fondled Mark, conflicting emotions running through her brain. She wanted to bend over and put it in her mouth, but she also wanted to get up and run back upstairs to Sarah. They had made love just minutes ago, each hungrily licking each other's pussies, but neither one could make the other cum. Finally, after what seemed like forever, they pulled away from each other unfulfilled. Sarah had laid on the bed, refusing to talk about it, and said she was going to take a nap, so Marissa had walked into the hall and peeked into Mark and Sophia's room.

The only other cock that she had touched was that of Darren Miller in tenth grade. She had invited him over to her house at the urging of her best friend, who knew that Darren liked her. With a few hours before her parents came home, he had made his move. He was nervous, but not as nervous as she was.

At that point in time, she was scared to think about what her life would be like as a lesbian, so she desperately wanted to like penis. Darren's cock had been almost laughably hard, the head nearly purple, and when he urged her to suck it, she did just that.

He lasted about fifteen seconds in her mouth before he grabbed her head in both hands and shoved his erupting cock into the back of her throat. She remembered the feeling of it gagging her, choking her, bile rising up in the back of her throat, threatening to come spraying out around his member. She remembered the taste of his semen, hot, salty and bitter, and so sticky and thick it clogged her throat.

She remembered struggling to pull away, slapping and clawing at his thighs. When she was sure that she was about to pass out, he pushed her away, his still hard cock waving in the air, more cum leaking out and running down the shaft. She saw it all clearly, it was etched in her brain, as she coughed and retched and tried to spit the offending mess into her hand.

It was the last time she ever wanted to see a penis again in her life, and she decided at that point that she didn't care what her parents thought anymore, she was a lesbian through and through.

Now, as she sat here next to Mark, her hand on his soft moist penis, she just wanted it in her mouth, shooting it's semen down her throat. Why she wanted it was a mystery to her, but it was all she could think about ever since she finished eating the pie. When she had peeked into his bedroom, she saw his wife doing what she wanted to do and her pussy was throbbing just seeing it.

"Marissa, do you want to suck it?" Mark asked.

Never taking her eyes off it, Marissa nodded her head.

"Go ahead then, put it in your mouth."

After a brief hesitation, Marissa slowly leaned forward. Her mouth was watering like she was about to eat a T-bone steak.

As she got closer, her lips were trembling as she opened her mouth and engulfed his flaccid penis. As soon as she felt it against her tongue, her pussy clenched with excitement and she squeezed her lips around it and started to suck.

It didn't take long after Marissa started to suck for Mark's cock to swell up to its full length. She had thick, soft lips and what she lacked in technique, she made up for in enthusiasm. Her tongue was fluttering all over the helmet shaped head, while her lips worked up and down and her hand gripped the shaft.

Even though Mark had just recently had an orgasm with his wife upstairs, it felt so different and good, that he was certain he would be able to cum again. After several minutes of Marissa working his erection though, he was really feeling the effects of too much stimulation, and he wasn't so sure that he would be able to cum.

Tiring quickly, Marissa pulled her mouth off Mark's tool and looked up at him. "Are you almost there Mark? Would you like me to take out my breasts?" She asked in a breathless voice.

Of course he wanted to see her breasts, he loved big soft breasts and the only reason that he hadn't asked her earlier, was the fact that he felt guilty about it being his daughters girlfriend. Now though, he was too horny to worry about Sarah. "Oh fuck yeah." he replied, just as breathless as Marissa.

Moving quickly, her embarrassment seemingly gone, Marissa pulled her tight top of over her head. Underneath, she was wearing a purple lace bra that seemed to be straining under the weight of her massive breasts. She reached behind her back and effortlessly unlatched the strap, (a feat of blind dexterity that always impressed Mark) then pulled her arms tightly to her sides, which held the now loose garment up. She glanced at Mark again with a shy grin and flutter of her eyes, before her eyes locked onto his erection again and she let the bra drop down her arms to the floor.

Marissa reached for Mark's saliva coated cock and began to stroke it when he decided to take control. "Marissa, kneel down on the floor in front of me." He waited while she followed his instruction, then said "Now put it between your tits."

Marissa looked up at him with furrowed brow, but she still moved forward and wrapped her breasts around his cock. They were so big that it nearly disappeared between them, only the head sticking out below her neck.

"Now squeeze 'em together and go up and down. You can suck the head while you do that too." Mark instructed.

She pushed the outside of her breasts together, creating a snug crevice between her two fleshy pillows, and tilted her head so she could catch his spongy head between her lips. She started to slide up and down and settled on just keeping her mouth open and her tongue out so when she slid down she could slide her tongue over the underside of his penis. As she found her rhythm, her saliva dripped down his shaft, making the passage slick and increasing his sensation.

"Oh shit that's fucking hot!" Mark groaned as he watched the large busted woman.

"Mark? Marissa? What the fuck is going on?!?"

Mark looked up at Sarah who was standing beside the couch. "Sarah, I..."

"Oh my God Mark, what are you doing?!?" Sarah yelled, her face a mask of confusion and anger. "Marissa, you..."

At that, Marissa finally pulled away from Mark's slicked up penis, and turned toward Sarah. "I can't help it Sarah, I need his cum." Her hand gripped his still hard cock.

Sarah looked like she was going to throw up, until her eyes lit upon Mark's cock. A dreamy look suddenly came over her, her eyes glazed over and she licked her lips.

"Sarah, are you alright?" Mark asked.

"Wh...oh shi..." Sarah blinked and looked away. "I...I can't believe you two. How could you do this?"

Marissa got to her feet and went to Sarah, putting her arm around her waist and saying "Sarah please, I don't know what happened."

"It's the pie isn't it Mark? Sophia said that the pie is cursed or something. Some Gypsy woman did something to the pie right? Sophia said she was going to see her." Sarah said, looking back at Mark but avoiding looking at his penis.

"Yes honey, it was the pie. It was for your mother. I didn't know you were coming home."

"So you brought home a pie that a crazy gypsy woman put a hex on for Sophia to eat. A pie that would make her want to...to perform fellatio on you."

"I know it sound crazy, but I think the woman might have hypnotised me or something. She's a witch I think." Mark said, realizing just how ridiculous this all sounded.

"Well, I can forgive you Marissa because you were basically drugged. Sophia went to find the woman and take care of this mess, so we just need to wait until she gets back."

"Sarah, I went to see her this morning when I saw that you had both eaten the pie. She told me there is nothing she can do. It's too late."

"I don't believe you. Sophia will take care of it, she has to." Sarah said. She was trying to stay strong, but Mark could see that she was struggling. "C'mon Marissa, let's wait upstairs." She turned and started to move toward the stairs, but Marissa stayed still.

"I can't." Marissa said, her voice wavering. "I need to finish Sarah. I need it." She got back down on her knees in front of Mark and grasped his shrinking cock.

Sarah looked back "Marissa...please come with me." Once again she looked at her Marks penis and her knees nearly buckled. She was weak, her mouth watering and her pussy throbbing.

"Sarah, you know you want it too." Marissa said waving Mark's suddenly ridged cock in the air enticingly. "Come try it. You'll love it."

"Nooooo" Sarah whined, but she was inching forward, her legs seemingly moving on their own accord.

Mark could see the struggle she was going through and it was brutal to watch. "Honey, it's alright. Take what you need, you'll feel better."

Marissa reached up and took Sarah by the hand, tugging her down until she was kneeling next to her between Mark's legs. "Go ahead babe, try it. It's sooo good." She said sliding her hand up and down the underside of Mark's penis.

Sarah tried to avert her eyes but they kept being drawn back. She couldn't bring herself to touch it though, until Marissa finally took her hand and placed it where the shaft turns into scrotum. The touch sent a tremor through Sarah's body. Once her hand was on Mark's penis, she couldn't take it off. Within moments she was sliding her hand up and down the hard shaft alongside Marissa's hand.

"Put it in your mouth Sarah." Marissa whispered. "Go ahead and try it. I know you want to."

Sarah looked at her girlfriend Marissa and pursed her lips. She was shaking her head no and the look in her eyes was one of utter terror, but she couldn't pull her hand away and with Marissa nodding her head she felt her will was breaking.

Mark was fascinated by the inner turmoil that his beautiful

friend was now going through. He felt bad to see her like this, but it was also something to see. He watched Marissa slowly convince her to try putting it in her mouth.

"I can't, it's so wrong." Sarah whined, but she made the mistake of looking at the shaft that she was still holding, and her eyes glazed over. She was mesmerized by the sight of it and she licked her lips again. That was when Marissa put her hand on the back of Sarah's head and gently pushed her forward.

Sarah had given up and didn't resist when her girlfriend pushed her head forward. As her lips came into contact with the shaft, a mini orgasm shook her to her core, and she gave in to the feelings and sucked the head into her mouth.

Meanwhile, on the other side of town, Sophia walked into the 'Witches Brew Potions' shop, intent on solving this dilemma that she found herself in. After her incredible orgasm with her husband, she laid on the bed recuperating and thinking about what he had told her. His story had been so ludicrous, that she was sure it wasn't true.

Sophia got up, put on a robe, and went to Sarah's room to get some information. She knocked on the door and opened it, walking in to find her daughter lying naked on the bed, and looking upset. Sarah covered herself and invited her Sophia in.

It took some prodding, but eventually Sarah broke down and told Sophia that she was having some really messed up 'daydreams' as she called them. She wouldn't tell her what the daydreams were about until Sophia told her about what Mark had told her earlier, then she started to cry hysterically and said that she was having those same visions of sucking his penis.

Armed with this new knowledge, Sophia now knew that what Mark had told her was the truth, and she vowed to take care of it. She told Sarah to go find Marissa and keep her away from Mark. "I'll go find this gypsy bitch and give her a piece of my mind." She told her.

Now, as she marched into the small shop, her anger seething, she was ready to tear into this gypsy woman and insist that she do something about this mess. She didn't bother to look around when the bell over the door jangled, she marched right up to the counter and announced herself. "Hello!!! I need someone out here right now!!!"

The curtain was pushed aside and Sophia looked into the eyes of the most beautiful woman she had ever seen. Now Sophia was not at all attracted to women, but when she looked into this woman's deep blue eyes, like pools of crystal clear water, she found herself at a loss for words.

"Hello ma'am, how can I help you?" The stunning beauty asked.

"Uhh, I um, I need to uh talk to you about..." She was lost all of a sudden, as if she couldn't remember at all the reason she had come into this cozy little shop at all.

"It's quite alright ma'am, just look into my eyes and I will know what you need." Her voice was silky smooth and sexy.

"Oookaaay." Sophia said in a drawn out drawl. This all seemed so dreamlike to her.

For the next ten minutes, Sophia stared into the endless eyes of the fiery redhead, her trance going deeper and deeper, until finally the gypsy pulled away. Sophia blinked rapidly several times and listened to what the lady behind the counter told her.

"I see that you have a dilemma that you need solved, is that correct ma'am?"

"Y - yes"

"I think that I have the only possible solution to your problem ma'am, but you'll need to follow me into the back room so I can mix a potion." She watched as Sophia made her way around the end of the counter and then held open the curtain for her.

Sophia walked into the back room, noticing that it seemed much too large for the small building. She was led to a small cot and told to strip all her clothes off. She was still in a trance, but her mind was not totally gone, so she asked why she needed to be naked.

"I know that it sounds odd ma'am, but in order to make my potion, I need some of your...womanly juices."

Surely she couldn't be serious, thought Sophia, there's no way in hell that I'm getting undressed in front of this strange woman. That's what her brain was telling her, but when she looked down, she realized that her pants were down around her ankles and she was pulling them off. Her body was moving on its own accord and while she tried to clear her muddled mind, she completely stripped off all her clothes.

It was alarming in a way how she wasn't in control of her own faculties, but at the same time she had a feeling of safety, that this strange but beautiful woman would take care of her and that all her needs would be met. She was strangely at ease, a total turnaround from the way she walked in to the store.

Sophia was led to an old cot up against the back wall, where she was instructed to lay down. She watched as the sexy gypsy woman took her ankles in her hands and spread her legs wide, then crawled up between her legs and began licking her pussy.

This was something that Mark had tried to do with her a few times, but she could never allow herself to enjoy the feeling because she was always so tense when he tried. It all stemmed back to when she was a child in school. Her family was poor so she was forced to wear second hand clothes that didn't always fit her too well. She was picked on and bullied a whole lot because of it, and she grew up with an internal dialog that still, to this day, told her that she was not good enough. She still loved Mark, but his indiscretions caused her to think that she wasn't good enough for him also.

The fact that it was a woman who was now licking her pussy was another thing that should have disturbed Sophia. Her thoughts about lesbianism had changed somewhat since finding out about her own friend, whom she loved unconditionally, but she still felt it was inherently wrong.

For some reason though, all this was turning Sophia on. The feeling of the gypsy woman's soft silky tongue fluttering around her clitoris was just heavenly, and when she felt the sexy young woman sliding something inside her pussy, her excitement increased.

Hands slid under Sophia's thighs and up her torso, causing her waist to be lifted up, her legs hanging over her, and her ass tilted forward. The hands continued, one on each side, massaging their way up her rib cage and ending up on her breasts, which swelled when she sucked in a great lungful of air. Fingers and thumbs went to work on each nipple, gently pinching and tugging, making her brown, sensitive nubs of flesh stand tall.

Opening her eyes, Sophia looked down at the gypsies eyes peering up at her from above her pubis. Those incredible, intense eyes, the windows into her soul, were somehow changing the inner dialog in Sophia's head, replacing the taunts and hurtful jokes with understanding and love and desire.

Sophia could feel something sliding deep into her vagina, much deeper than any humans tongue was capable of reaching, but she somehow knew that it was the gypsies tongue that was worming around inside her, like a long wet snake that was trained to know all the right spots to cause just the right amount pleasure. She knew it was her tongue because the woman's hands were on her breasts while her mouth was plastered over her vulva, sucking her entire pussy with gusto.

The fact that she could feel this impossibly long tongue gliding around inside her, reaching places that her husband's penis had never reached, should have alarmed Sophia enough to send her running away, but instead, it seemed like the most rational thing that she could be doing at this time.

Then she felt the slippery eel shaped organ touch a place inside her that she never knew existed. She had heard talk about the G spot in women and always thought it was nothing more than propaganda to sell magazines, but now she was having second thoughts about that as she felt this indescribable pleasure building up inside her.

Sophia was going to cum, and the feeling that she had last night and earlier today with Mark, the feeling that she was going to urinate, was back. The first two times she felt the feeling when she came, she was unable to control it and she wound up drenching her bed. It hadn't seemed to bother Mark and after her powerful orgasms, she was too worn out to worry about it either. Now however, she had a woman whose mouth was attached to her pussy and didn't seem to be ready to move anytime soon.

"Oh my God I'm gonna cum, you should move!" Sophia managed to breathlessly tell the woman, whose eyes narrowed to slits as if she was grinning widely. The snaking appendage inside her continued its assault on her G spot and she gripped the sides of the cot with her hands as the orgasm took hold of her.

Sarah couldn't believe that she was on her knees sucking on the head of Marks's penis. This was not supposed to happen, something that she would have never believed if she hadn't been having these crazy visions of him naked, his swollen cock dripping juices that made her pussy throb and her mouth water.

She had been so upset with herself for having these visions and had tried to put them out of her head by fooling around with Marissa, but it hadn't worked at all. No matter how hard they both tried, neither one of them could get the other to cum, and when Marissa started acting weird, Sarah got scared that something was wrong.

So she had talked to her Sophia about it and Sophia had told her all about the pie from the gypsy woman. It made her skin crawl to think that Mark could do something like that. Sophia had said to stay as far away from Mark as possible, but when she went looking for Marissa, her worst fears were realized. She meant to get her girlfriend out of there, but instead, she found herself doing the one thing that she was sure she wouldn't do.

The penis in her mouth, her father's penis, was giving her strange but delectable feelings in her pussy, and while it was in her mouth, she was happier than she had ever been in her entire life. It was like this was what she was meant to do, and she was going to continue sucking this cock until it spewed its life, its essence into her mouth, and she would swallow all that he offered and be content.

As for Mark, he could see that Sarah had no more qualms about what she was doing, and that made him feel somewhat better, but he wondered how she was going to feel after they finished. Right now though, he was just enjoying the wonderful feelings and the sight of two sexy women both trying to devour his cock, even though one of the women happened to be his wife's very best friend.

Things were getting serious now as Sarah and Marissa were both sucking on Mark's cock together. Sarah would suck the head while Marissa was tonguing and sucking the sack, then they would switch. While they were both working on Mark's cock, they were also rubbing each other's sopping wet pussies. They were both moaning and whining and it was so fucking hot that Mark was quickly worked up to the edge of orgasm.

"Oh shit girls, I'm almost there. I'm gonna cum." Mark groaned.

Sarah, upon hearing that he was going to cum, grabbed his shaft and held it straight up. Marissa moved up and both girls put their lips on the head together, as if they were kissing each other with a penis between them. Sarah even felt the first shot of semen traveling up his shaft, before squirting up between the two sets of lips. Both girls got a good taste and they both immediately began to cum also, their pussies both squirting a fair amount of juices and filling the room with the unmistakable smell of sex.

The two girls both did their best to share the entire load and when Mark's cock finally stopped spewing its load, they each licked the remains off each other's lips and cheeks, and finished by passionately kissing each other while they knelt in their own juices.

Shuddering and moaning, her muscles clenching through erotic spasms, Sophia rode through her third extreme orgasm in two days, the very first one ever brought on by another woman. Although the two orgasms that she enjoyed with her husband had been incredible, they occurred with little or no stimulation. This one was all due to stimulation, and the stimulation was like none she had ever experienced.

Not wanting to spray her juices while the gypsy woman was still down there sucking and tickling her insides with an impossibly long tongue, Sophia tried to hold back, but with her G spot being massaged so expertly, she couldn't have held it in if she wanted and she felt and heard her powerful spray forcing its way past the snakelike appendage inside her. She wanted it to stop and she never wanted it to stop.

Cumming so hard, Sophia lifted up her head and looked back into the gypsy woman's eyes. The eyes seemed as if they were glowing red, surely it must have been a trick of the light, but it was rather unsettling.

Sophia was spraying so hard and it was all going into the woman's mouth. As good as her orgasm felt, it was also the most draining orgasm she ever had. It seemed as if her energy was all spraying out of her pussy with her juices, and she had a moment where she envisioned the gypsy as a vampire who drained a person's life force through their genitals. Certainly a ridiculous notion to be sure, but the pie had seemed ridiculous too.

When her orgasm finished, Sophia felt so drained that she could barely keep her eyes open. What she saw seemed like it must have been a dream. She felt the tongue sliding out of her pussy before the gypsy pulled her face away from her pussy. It was what she saw next that was so dreamlike, that she would later question if she really had seen it. The gypsy woman's cheeks were blown up like a balloon all the way to her neck. They seemed impossibly large, and she struggled to keep her eyes open long enough to watch the woman pick up an ornate bottle and spit the entire contents of her mouth into it.

Exhausted, Sophia fell into a deep sleep.

The next thing Sophia knew, she was back in the first room in the shop standing at the counter. Her clothes were back on and she wondered if it all had been a dream. The curtain was pushed aside and out stepped an old frail looking woman with the deepest wrinkles lining her face. She was carrying an ornate bottle that was stopped with a cork and Sophia thought it looked strangely familiar, but couldn't remember where she had seen it.

"Okay dear," The old decrepit woman said in a gravelly voice, "now to help you with your problem, you need to make sure that all the women who ate the pie take a drink from this bottle, including you. You should finish all the drink in here to make sure that it will never wear off. Also, I have something that you should give to your husband. I tried to give it to him earlier when he came in, but he left too soon."

The old woman reached down below the counter and pulled out a strange looking root and placed it on the counter. Sophia could tell it was a root because it resembled a carrot with a green stem sticking up from one end and several leaves coming off the stem. But the root was definitely not a carrot. For one, it was not orange, but the color of skin, and it was not shaped like a carrot, it looked exactly like an erect penis, with veins and a mushroom shaped head.

"It is very important that your husband drinks the juices that are inside this root, no matter how much he balks at doing it, if you need to force him, then force him, but make sure he drinks all the juices inside here. He should put this end in his mouth and suck it like a straw until nothing more comes out."

Sophia picked up the root and felt it. It was warm and the 'skin' felt remarkably similar to a man's penis. She looked into the old woman's face and asked "What is this thing?"

"It is mentula olus, and it will give your husband the strength he is going to need for this. It is imperative that you see to it that he takes this."

As strange as all this seemed to Sophia, and after everything that she had gone through and witnessed, she should have asked more questions, but she was still in a fog about what had happened since she had arrived, and she was still in a hypnotic like trance. She picked up the bottle in one hand and the root was still in her other hand, and left the shop on still shaky legs.

When Sophia arrived back at her home, she carried the bottle and strange penis shaped root directly to the kitchen. She hid the root in a rarely opened cupboard up over the refrigerator before popping the cork on the bottle. She took out three tall glasses and poured equal amounts in all three glasses until the bottle was empty. Each glass was nearly half full with the murky fluid.

She picked up one glass and smelled it. It smelled like female musk, not something that she wanted to just hand to her daughter and her daughter's girlfriend. She went to the fridge and pulled out the jug of iced tea, then capped off each glass with the cold sweet tea. She took out a long spoon and stirred each glass, then smelled one of them again. Now it smelled like nothing more than iced tea. Picking the glass up, she drank the concoction down.

After finishing the entire contents of the glass, she set the glass in the sink and burped. It had tasted like iced tea with a hint of something else. Not feeling at all different from before she drank the stuff, she decided to go find the girls and have them drink the rest.

Sophia found the two girls sitting together in the den, and upon seeing them, she was struck by how sexy they both looked. A vivid picture of Sarah and Marissa naked and making love to each other flashed through Sophia's brain and she felt her pussy twitch. She closed her eyes and shook her head, pushing the images out of her mind, and wondering why she was thinking like that.

"Hi girls, would you both come with me to the kitchen please." Sophia asked and waited for them to get up and follow her. She wondered if they had both managed to stay away from Mark and for some reason, she hoped that they hadn't.

Once in the kitchen she said "I have something that you both need to drink. It's from the gypsy, and she seemed real concerned when I told her about our predicament. She mixed up this drink right in front of me and told me that we all need to drink it. I already drank my glass and it tastes just like iced tea."

"What is it supposed to do Sophia?" Sarah asked.

"It should take care of our problem honey, and listen, you

shouldn't feel bad, either one of you, if you did anything with Mark already, it's not your fault at all."

"Thanks Sophia." Sarah said and looked at Marissa "Okay, let's do this."

Both girls began drinking the potion until both glasses were empty. Once finished, both girls burped and giggled before setting their glasses in the sink.

"Am I supposed to feel any different Mrs. Stanley?" Marissa asked.

"Well, do you?" Sophia returned the question.

After a moment or two of thought, Marissa replied "I don't know, not really." And she didn't really feel any different either, she thought to herself, as she admired how sexy her girlfriends friend really was and wished they were all naked.

"How about you Sarah? Do you feel any different?" Sophia questioned.

Sarah shrugged and shook her head back and forth slowly, but her mind was picturing what her best friend would look like naked and she wondered what her pussy would taste like.

"Okay girls, I've got one more thing that I need to do, and I may need your help." Sophia went to the cupboard where she had hidden the root and pulled it out. "This is a special root that is supposed to help Mark, but I don't think that he will want to take it."

"What do you have to do, fuck him with it?" Sarah asked, looking at the penis shaped root.

"No, he has to suck the juices out of it and swallow them."

Sarah smiled a devious smile and said "Don't worry Sophia, I know just what we can do to convince him to do that."

Mark had left the basement after watching Sarah and her girlfriend share his sperm. He needed a workout to clear his head of all the shit that had happened. Upstairs was his workout room where he had a treadmill, weight system, stationary bike, and other tools of the trade. He spent the next 45 minutes working up a sweat.

He was interrupted by his wife calling from down the hall. "Honey, can you please come to the bedroom. I need you right away."

"Yeah, I'll be right there." He called back, mopping up the sweat from his forehead with a towel. He hopped off the stationary bike and headed down the hallway to the bedroom. Walking into the bedroom, Mark froze two steps in when he saw the sight of Sarah and Marissa both naked on his bed.

Thinking that Sophia must be in another room, Mark said "Uh sorry girls." and he turned around, bumping right into his wife, also nude. "Jesus what th..." he said, momentarily startled. "Honey, what the fuck is going on?" He asked backing up slowly as she moved toward him.

"We just all want to show you how much we appreciate everything that you have done for us honey." Sophia answered, advancing on him sexily.

"What have I done for you?" He was getting just a bit scared at the way they were all acting.

"You have opened up all our minds to carnal pleasures that we never knew before. We owe you so much for that." Sophia said, as she continued to advance upon a retreating Mark.

Mark could tell there was something very wrong with the way they all were acting. He knew that Sophia had gone to the shop, so that was where he started. "What happened to you at the shop?" He asked his wife as she was trying to pull at his clothes. He stepped back one more time and his legs came upon the foot of the bed.

"Girls, take him down." Sophia said evenly, and before Mark could react, his arms were grabbed from behind by both girls and Sophia pushed onto him using her whole body. With both girls pulling back on his arms and his wife tackling him, he had no chance and found himself on his back with his wife astride him, her full weight on his chest.

"What the hell are you doing?" He was worried now as the girls pulled his arms up over his head and held him like that. Mark was a fairly strong guy, but the way they had him, he had no leverage to pull his arms down. Plus there was the fact that he had just finished his workout, a particularly strenuous workout at that, and he was too tired and sore to muster any strength.

"I'm going to help you Mark," Sophia answered, "just like I helped Sarah and Marissa earlier."

"What do you mean?" He looked up at Sarah and Marissa and yelled "What did she do to you?!?"

"Oh relax will you. I just gave them a drink that I got from your friend over at the potion shop. I guess I thought that it was going to take our cravings for your semen away, but it seems to have not worked. We all still want your cock and cum Mark. So I guess that her stuff didn't work this time, but that's okay, because she showed me some incredible things Mark. When she licked my pussy and stuck her tongue up inside me, I thought I would never stop cumming. It was so fucking good, and now that I know how fun it is to fuck women, I'm not holding back anymore. I realize now why our little girls here likes pussy so much."

It was obvious to Mark that Sophia had already been changed by whatever the gypsy woman did to her, so he tried to reason with Sarah instead. "Sarah honey, let me up. Can't you see that this is not the way Sophia acts? That woman did something to her, she's been brainwashed or something."

What Sarah said next sent a chill down Mark's spine. "It's okay Mark, Sophia just wants me and Marissa and her to all be lovers now, and I want it too." He realized that all three of them had been changed, and he was helpless to stop them from doing whatever they wanted right now.

Mark tried to reason with Sophia once more. "Listen hon, you are my wife and I am so sorry that I did this to you, but you need to fight this. You know deep down that this is wrong, this is not what any of you want. Let me up and we can all go together to see the gypsy. We can demand that she take this curse away…"

"Curse?!?" Sophia barked "This is no curse Mark. This is enlightenment. Look, all you need to do is suck on this root like it's a straw, and you will find out." She held up the penis shaped root in front of Mark's face.

It looked like a seven inch penis attached to some kind of plant. Mark shook his head back and forth "No fucking way am I putting that in my mouth." He said defiantly.

"Oh we will see about that, won't we."

Mark could feel the girls moving around on his arms while still keeping him pinned down. At first he didn't know what they were doing, and when he realized what they had done, it was too late. They climbed off his now bound arms and moved to his legs which were still planted on the floor. Mark looked up at his arms which were now tied together. The other end of the rope was tied tightly to the headboard. He tested the knots and the strength of the rope and found out that it was tightly tied and very strong.

While he was testing the ropes holding his arms, he became aware of his legs being pulled apart, stretched to either side of the bed, and realized too late that they were also tied. "Shit! Let me up." He snapped, but Sophia didn't move off his chest.

"Not until you suck this like a straw." She smiled a creepy smile.

His arms and legs bound and helpless now, the two nude girls used a pair of scissors to start cutting off all of Mark's workout clothes. One pulled off his sneakers and socks while the other cut his shorts and underwear off until he was naked from the waist down. The scissors were then passed to Sophia, who began to cut off his muscle shirt.

Naked and at their mercy, Mark next asked "Okay, so now what? I'm not letting you put that in my mouth and I'm certainly not going to suck on it if you do. So now what are you going to do? You got me naked, so now what?"

"Sarah reminded me earlier how much you hate to be tickled Mark. You said once that being tickled is like being tortured, only worse, because you can handle pain but you can't handle being tickled. Remember when you said that Mark?"

He did remember. It was a time when he and Sophia were being playful a few years ago and wrestling in the living room. Sarah had come to her friends rescue and the two of them had used tickling to make Mark cry. It was all just in fun and they all laughed about it, but later at the dinner table, Mark confessed to being hopelessly ticklish, and said that when he was a boy, he had been held down by his older brother and tickled until he peed himself. They all laughed at the story, but Mark had said that he really hated being tickled.

Sophia saw the reaction in her husband's face and continued "You will not only suck this root Mark, but you will beg me to allow you to suck this root. It may take an hour, or two hours, hell it may take all day long even. We don't care how long it takes Mark, we can wait. We are going to see just how ticklish you really are honey, and when you have had enough, you will beg me to let you suck this. Then we will stop."

"Jesus Sophia, don't do this. Sarah, Marissa, let me up, please, you don't want this. It's not...ffffuucckkk ha ha hah haa ha ssstoppp no no no don't ahh hah ha ha haaaaa!!!"

All three woman were attacking him from every different angle. Marissa was tickling both his feet at the same time, running her fingertips back and forth along the soft underside. Sarah had sat up on his upper arms and was tickling his armpits, while his wife was sitting on his limp penis and attacking his sides.

To Mark, it was the worst torture that they could dish out and he was going wild trying unsuccessfully to get away. He was laughing uncontrollably, losing his breath and gasping, tears pouring from his eyes, while he tried to get out a few clear words.

"Ahhssstohhp sstohhp huh nn ha ha ha ahh nooo don't huu ah haha!!" He was yanking his hands painfully hard, but still was not able to get loose.

While Sophia was digging her fingers into Mark's sides, she noticed that his cock was growing under her ass. "Hey girls, look at this." She said, stopping her tickling to stand up and show them that his cock was standing straight up. "He likes this. Let's give him more."

They had all stopped for a second or two to see and Mark, still gasping said "W- wait, just wait. N -no more."

Sophia slid his erect penis into her pussy. She was plenty wet and had been ever since she finished drinking the iced tea concoction. "Are you ready to suck the root?" She asked, holding it up again and putting it just above his mouth.

"What huh what is it huh going to do huh to me?" Mark was breathing so hard he was huffing.

"Well, I'm not sure honey, but we can find out in a hurry if you just suck it." Sophia said.

"Please no more tickling. I'll do it, just stop the tickling please."

"Oh you'll do it will you. Well you need to beg me to let you suck it."

As bad as it would be, Mark was certain that he couldn't take anymore tickling, so in defeat he said "Please, let me suck on the root."

"Open up" Sophia ordered, and when he did, she placed the cock shaped root in her husband's mouth. She watched him close his lips around the head and then pretend to suck on it. It was a pathetic acting job and she dug her fingers into his side again and yelled "Suck it!".

Mark was almost surprised by the warmth of the phallic looking root. It felt alive in his mouth and he moved his lips up and down in an attempt to trick his wife. When she dug her fingers into his side again and yelled 'suck it', he involuntarily began sucking. It was only a little bit, but that was all it took. One tiny suck and a tiny bit of warm fluid squirted into his mouth. It was a bitter tasting fluid that had a weird effect on his mouth, it caused him to pucker, which in turn caused him to suck more which caused much more fluid to squirt into his mouth. He wasn't in control of his mouth anymore and couldn't stop sucking if he wanted to.

It took about twenty seconds before the root was empty and it took another twenty seconds before Mark got control of his mouth enough to stop sucking and spit the thing out. He hadn't even noticed that he was cumming inside his wife's pussy while he was swallowing the fluid.

Sophia noticed though that his cock was going soft inside her and when she slid off, a glob of white cum leaked from her pussy onto his leg. The two girls who had earlier shared his cum, both moved on it quickly. Marissa being on the floor got to it first and licked the slime off his leg before engulfing his flaccid cock in her mouth and sucking the remaining fluid off, moaning and cumming the whole time.

Sarah looked on in disappointment as she still needed to eat more of her Marks cum, but Sophia, seeing her friend's sad face said "Come here honey and suck it out of me." She spun around on the bed and spread her legs wide.

Without a second thought or a worry about it being her bestie, Sarah dove down and clamped her lips around her pussy. She started to suck and was rewarded with a stream of cum oozing into her mouth. "Mmmm" she moaned as she swallowed the mess and continued to suck, her own pussy going into spontaneous spasms of orgasm.

Just then, Marissa gasped and picked her head up. "Look, he's hard again!" She announced and sure enough Mark's overused cock was standing erect again.

"It must be the root. The gypsy told me that it would give you the strength you would need for this. That was what she meant, that you would have the strength to satisfy all three of us from now on."

Sarah pulled her mouth off her mother's pussy and said "Well then let's give it a try."

Mark was unsure what was going on and was surprised that his cock was still hard, but then the strangest thing happened, Sarah took his cock, wrapped her lips around it, and sucked, and he started to cum again. It wasn't exactly what he would call an orgasm though because it felt a bit like he was peeing, but after a few moments, Sarah picked up her head and said "It's wonderful, he's cumming so much."

Marissa put her lips around his little head next and sucked, and was rewarded with a blast of semen which she swallowed down. She slid her lips back until just the very tip of Mark's penis was still between them and sucked as if she was sucking soda through a straw. Her hand wrapped around his shaft felt the viscous fluid flowing as she sucked and swallowed.

It was a very strange feeling for Mark as the two girls drained his balls. It wasn't an uncomfortable feeling, but there was little to no pleasure involved. A few seconds later, when his wife took his cock and sucked half of his length into her mouth, he felt the pleasure of the blowjob, but she stopped after sucking a mouthful of his cum.

Mark was left tied to the bed while the three women, his wife, her friend and her lesbian lover, all had sex together. He couldn't believe how they were all acting like what they were doing was the most natural thing in the world. His wife was the one who surprised him the most though, because she had always been so turned off by lesbians.

He watched as Marissa lay above him on the bed, her legs spread wide and held open by her arms, while Sarah knelt on the floor in front of her licking and sucking her pussy. Meanwhile, not to be outdone, Mark's wife Sophia, who had always been turned off by lesbians, was on her knees behind her, licking away at her ass. It was a disturbing but highly erotic scene.

For the next hour, while Mark begged to be set free, the three women fingered, fisted, licked, sucked and fucked each other to several screaming orgasms. About half way through their orgy, Sophia grew tired of listening to Mark's whining and she crammed a pair of her daughter's underwear into his mouth. She used a soiled pair of her nylons to gag him so he wouldn't be able to spit out the undies, then she re-joined the orgy.

Epilogue

After a long weekend of lesbian sex between the three women, Sarah and Marissa both decided that they didn't really need to return to college after all, and they moved in with Mark and Sophia for good.

The more the three women were together, the more depraved their actions became. It seemed as if the iced tea mixture had taken away all their inhibitions, leaving them willing to try anything that came to mind, no matter how degrading or perverted it was. They became extremely familiar with every inch of each other's bodies and there was never an ounce of jealousy between them.

Watching the three women closely, Mark noticed that they all seemed to become intoxicated by each other's womanly smells. Things that they would have looked at as gross or disgusting in the past, was now highly erotic to all three. For instance, they seemed to get aroused by sniffing each other's armpits, feet, and asses. They would also smell each other's soiled underwear and get aroused by the musky scent.

Mark was getting frustrated at being used as nothing more than a drinking fountain by all three women who now lived in his home. It seemed to Mark like the only thing the women were interested in anymore was each other's bodies. They all came to see him every day to get their fill of semen that they craved, but then they wanted to have sex with each other, leaving Mark to sit on the side-lines and watch. He would get so turned on by watching that he would masturbate, but that didn't seem to work anymore.

He would often wake up to one of the girls sucking the head of his cock and swallowing the semen that just flowed out of it. It always felt good, but they would never continue until he could actually feel an orgasm.

He made a return trip back to the potion shop a few days later. The beautiful, sexy gypsy smiled and welcomed him. He had prepared himself for this moment, and even though he struggled to keep his mind from turning into a pile of mush, he managed to ask her what the potion was that she had given his wife.

The explanation she gave cleared everything up for Mark. She said that since there was no way to reverse the original potion, and all three women were going to keep coming to him every day for his sperm, she was concerned that there would be jealousy between them. The only solution was to give them something to take away all their inhibitions. The potion also would allow them all to sexually satisfy each other instead of them only getting their satisfaction from swallowing his sperm.

The root was something that would allow Mark to easily pump out plenty of sperm, enough to satisfy all three women every single day, and she assured him that he could still enjoy the pleasure associated with orgasm. He left the shop with answers and a small vial that she had given him. The potion inside, if he chose to take it, would loosen his inhibitions.

He decided to drink the potion a day later after watching his wife and Sarah in a heated 69 while Marissa stood behind Sophia licking her asshole. He was turned on by the scene, but he was tortured by the fact that it was his wife's friend who he was lusting over. After he swallowed the liquid in the vial, he walked over to his wife, pulled her head up, and shoved his swollen cock into Sarah's pussy. He kept pulling out and alternating between fucking her pussy and his wife's mouth. His plans for acquiring the old, dilapidated building for the land seemed unimportant now, and Mark retreated from the hustle and bustle of everyday life, opting instead to live off his acquired wealth.

The days that followed were filled with sex. All four of them stayed naked almost all the time while they were home and nothing was off limits. Their play was only limited by their imagination and with the Internet readily available, their imaginations never slowed. Every secret fantasy that any one of them ever considered was fair game now that they had no inhibitions, and all of them was more than willing to try anything new.